RAZ·MA·TAZ

Written By:
STEPHEN COSGROVE

Illustrated By
ROBIN JAMES

GROLIER ENTERPRISES INC.
Danbury, Connecticut

A Serendipity™ Book™

This book about a goat is dedicated to my good friend Chuck Gates because I'm always getting his.

Stephen

Beyond tomorrow, just this side of today, stands a magnificent range of mountains called the Highest of High. The mountains are so high that dawn and dusk seem to collide as the wind sweeps the clouds way up to the sky.

Below the peaks of the Highest of High are the misty, mountain meadows where the alpine flowers bend and sigh.

In these lush, green meadows of the Highest of High live many wondrous creatures. There are eagles who catch each dip in the wind and seem to soar forever without flapping a wing. There are boulder bunnies who hop about, twitching their noses in the air. And, most wondrous of all, there are goats of Highest of High.

The goats are short and fat with long grey and white fur that ruffles in the wind. They don't do much. Rather, they are content to graze about the meadows munching on a bite of grass or occasionally sniffing a flower or two.

All of the goats, that is, except one very special goat named Raz Ma Taz. Raz would spend all day racing about the meadows. He would bounce from rock to rock. Then he would run from one end of the meadow to the other just to see if the other goats would notice him. But the other goats would only look up as he zipped by and then continue their gentle munching of the green, green grass.

"Pooh, those old fuddy duddies wouldn't notice their own reflection in the water," Raz said as he raced off to the end of the meadow.

One day, as he was running about, he noticed the other goats watching the eagles soar on the wind. "Ah, ha!" he said. "Maybe if I flew like an eagle they would notice me." So he climbed atop a large boulder, jumped high into the air and madly flapped his legs. He stayed in the air for only a moment and, like a bag full of bricks, he fell to the ground with a thud. The other goats looked up for a moment and went back to their grazing.

"Hmmm!" Raz thought as he struggled to his feet, "maybe being an eagle isn't all it's cut out to be." He wandered about the meadow thinking and thinking of something else that would make the other goats notice him.

"Maybe if I just bumped one of them he'd notice me," he thought. So he bounced around once or twice, reared on his hind legs and rammed an old goat with his head.

The old goat stood there looking at Raz Ma Taz in total amazement. Then, with a 'whoof' he turned and butted Raz right on the rump, sending him flying. The other goats looked up, smiled their little goat smiles and continued their contented grazing.

Raz again picked himself up and hobbled about, his feelings more hurt than anything. "Golly!" he sobbed. "The only thing I want is to be noticed; instead I just get pushed around." With a large tear trickling from his eye he started to walk from the meadow.

He hadn't gone far when he heard someone giggling. Raz turned quickly toward the sound, but nothing was there except a large rock. Thinking it was only his imagination, he started to leave. Again he heard the laughter, and spinning quickly around he saw a whole group of boulder bunnies rolling around and laughing.

"What's so funny?" he asked gruffly.

"You looked so silly when you got butted that we just had to laugh," said the rabbits. And with that they again burst into gales of laughter.

"I'll show you what's silly about being butted!" he said as he slowly backed up. He then lowered his head and charged the bunnies who scampered nimbly out of the way. He looked around, saw more bunnies and charged again. As before the boulder bunnies easily hopped out of the way.

"Why you long-eared balls of fur!" Raz shouted as he charged at a bunch of bunnies standing right in front of a rock. Fortunately, the bunnies again bounded out of the way. Unfortunately, Raz, who had his head down and couldn't see where he was going, ran straight into the rock.

With his eyes all dazed and twisted he sat down with a thump. The rabbits skipped away chanting, "Silly goat, silly goat, ninner, ninner, ninner!"

For a while, Raz Ma Taz just sat there, feeling very sorry for himself. "Stupid goats! Stupid bunnies! I'll show them all. I'll run away." With a choked-back sob he ran into the foothills of the mountains of Highest of High.

Tears filled his eyes as he scampered along the narrow trail that led up the mountain, higher and higher.

He was so mad because no one had paid attention to him, that he didn't pay attention to the angry, dark clouds that were gathering in the skies.

Over rocks and under rocks Raz climbed higher and higher and higher. He would have kept climbing to the very top had it not been for a bright bolt of lightning and a loud clap of thunder.

It happened so quickly that he jumped off the edge of the path and landed right on top of a craggy boulder. He grabbed on to the rock as the thunder and lightning crashed around him.

Poor Raz looked about and realized that now there was no way to get down. The sky was snapping around him and far below he could see the other goats grazing in the meadow.

"Boy!" he said through chattering teeth. "They never paid attention to me before but I really wish they would pay attention to me now." He took a really deep breath and shouted "Help! Help!" The other goats looked up and smiled their little goat smiles and went right on munching the lush green grass.

"Oh, no! I've teased them so much before that they won't notice me now when I need them." And he began to cry soft, little tears.

He might have been hanging on that rock until this very day if the boulder bunnies hadn't realized that something was wrong. "You know," said one of the bunnies, "I think he's really in trouble."

They all looked up and because the bunnies were looking up, the goats also looked up and saw poor Raz high on the peak of the mountains of Highest of High.

"That little goat is in trouble and we've got to help," said the bunnies. They began hopping into the foothills with the goats right behind them.

They scampered up the mountain until they were on a ledge of rock right above Raz Ma Taz. "But how are we going to get him off the rock?" asked one of the rabbits.

The goats thought for a bit and just as another lightning bolt flashed, they came up with an idea. They told it to the bunnies and since there was no other plan, they all agreed.

One of the goats gently picked up one of the bunnies by the tail and slowly hung him over the edge. The next bunny climbed up on the goat's back, climbed over his head and down to the first bunny. Very carefully he grabbed his ears and then hung down even farther over the edge. One by one all the bunnies hung down on the bunny chain until the final bunny was right in front of Raz Ma Taz.

He was so shocked at seeing a bunny hanging there in mid-air that he didn't know what to do. "Put your arms around my waist," said the bunny "and we'll pull you to safety."

He did as he was told and then, with all the goats pulling and tugging, they lifted him to safety.

With Raz safely in the lead, all the bunnies and all the goats walked slowly down the trail from the Highest of High.

From that day forward Raz Ma Taz contentedly grazed in the misty meadows of the Mountain of the Highest of High. And whenever he felt that nobody was paying attention to him, he would lower his head, stomp his feet and gently bump a boulder.

IF YOU'RE SHOWING OFF
AND NO ONE PAYS ATTENTION
JUST REMEMBER RAZ MA TAZ
AND HIS SCARY REVELATION